TWO VOLUMES OF SHORT STORIES

THE DRESS

THE SHARDA STORIES

JESS WELLS

ALSO BY THE AUTHOR

Run, 1981

The Sharda Stories, 1982

A Herstory of Prostitution in Western Europe
(Shameless Hussy Press, Oakland, Calif.). 1982

The Dress, The Cry and A Shirt With No Seams,
first edition © 1984
second edition © 1985

Stories in this volume have appeared in "Common Lives/ Lesbian Lives" and "On Our Backs"

First edition by Library B Productions,
re-edited and revised, 1986
   ©1986 by Jess Wells. All Rights Reserved.

ISBN: 0-940721-00-7

Book Design: Tim Barrett, Studio de Boom
Cover Painting: "Spikes," by Laurie White
Jacket Photo: Helen Keller
Typesetting: Graphion

Published by Library B Productions
100 Valencia St., #119
San Francisco, CA 94103

Dedicated to Sharon, who knows that writing is a lifeline, not a hobby and love a gift, not a prize.

C O N T E N T S

The Dress 1

Why I Hate Poetry 9

The Cry 15

Sleeping Dogs 23

Marina 31

A Shirt With No Seams 45

Morning Girls 49

Gloria 63

The Succubus 71

The Sharda Stories 87

THE DRESS

THE DRESS

So, I'm in the thrift store after work; I'm smudged up with ink and my back hurts from running a printing press all day. Shopping has been mildly successful: I've found a wool sweater from Italy, a shirt for my lover and a 100% cotton bathrobe for myself. As I'm unloading my finds onto the counter for this dyke with a mustache and eye make-up to tally, I look up. There is this dress . . . hanging there (my neck freezes in a tilted position) . . . an incredible dress.

"Woa," I say to the dyke, who has seen my mouth open and is grinning while she looks at my tags. "So . . . how much is the dress?"

"Twenty-one fifty," she says, "It's a steal, believe me."

I look back at the bathrobe. Well, I'm glad it costs that much: I'm hardly going to spend 20 bucks on a dress.

But I can't take my eyes off it.

It's black. It's a work of art. It's a strapless, knee-length gown with a skirt like a pyramid, layers and layers of black shiny stuff (I don't know what you call it: I know cotton and I know flannel.) Anyway, black and then another layer of black and then gauze and net. Sewn onto the layers, in no kind of pattern, are these gorgeous hot pink poppies made of satin; little ones and big ones glowing in different intensities through the layers — not gaudy, mind you, "just a suggestion," as my mother would say. And then over the top of all of it and up the tight bodice to the breasts, is this black lace.

It's probably too small, I think, and besides, my 'hundred percent cotton bathrobe and such are all bagged up in front of me. It's time to go.

But instead, I say, "Here, will you keep these a minute?" and push the bag back, "I have to try on that dress."

Well, just then another worker takes the dress down for an older woman who is obviously buying it for someone else and there's a whole crowd of people standing around her because I'm telling you, it's a work of art, this dress. She's holding it up and women are fingering the layers and admiring the stitching. She's definitely decided to buy it.

Suddenly, I'm tapping her on the shoulder.

"May I try it on?"

"Certainly, dear, go right ahead," she says, giving me a motherly once-over.

Now, let me tell you very clearly that I am a dyke. I am not a gay lady or a homosexual woman, I am a fucking man-hating dyke. I do not look straight. I don't wear nice girl make-up or sweet-little suits or passable shoes. I am a fucking spikey-dyke. And this noisy dress, rustling even while it's cradled in my

The Dress

arms, is like a foreign object, like nothing I've ever touched before. I strip off my tank-top and my sweat pants and fuzzy crew socks and high-top Adidas. It probably won't fit, I think.

I slip it onto my naked body. I zip it up the back, very, very slowly. It's going to catch somewhere, this dress isn't really for me, I'm thinking.

It zips. To the top. And it's incredible, because that slinky material is lying in folds across my ass and I can feel the air rushing up to my cunt. There are these stays in the bodice that touch my ribs like fingers and I can feel the air coming down around my breasts, my breasts that touch against the sides of this lacy thing, pull away and then touch it again. I turn a circle and the layers fan out and slide across my ass: it feels like the tease of lifting the sheets up and laying them down again. What a dress. The top of me feels totally naked, even though I know it's not and my cunt feels buried beneath this black lace, ass feeling a fabric that only it knows about. My cunt, in the middle of 17 Reasons Why Thrift Store, is getting totally juiced out.

Oh Goddess, I'm thinking, I could wear it to a Sleaze Dance, with fingerless black gloves and big ol' chains, nasty, nasty make-up and spike heels. I could surprise my lover with it. I would drop her off at the door, tell her it was bad luck to see my costume first or some such excuse and she would complain and ask questions and try to have things her way as usual but I would insist.

Then, about a half hour later, when I was sure she had made the rounds and was standing with a beer and two or three friends, I would come in. Not, repeat, NOT, like a helpless femme-bot. Like a bad-ass, no-games, knows-her-mind-and-will-tell-you-too, femme. First, I would just stand there, and let her wonder. Maybe I would just stand there altogether, and let her come to me. Or maybe, while all the heads were turning (because of the dress, now, I'm not fooling myself) I would stride across the dance floor in a bee-line for that green-eyed woman I love, so that everyone would see who the one in that black dress was going to fuck tonight; everyone would see her frozen in her tracks, exposed, just like me. Standing in the thrift store dressing room, I can see her squirming. It's making my blood sing.

Now, I am one of those lesbians, who, unfortunately, was not born a lesbian; I didn't know at age five that I was queer. I spent (totally regrettable) years as a heterosexual and it made me very uncomfortable with any amount of beauty I might have. I pull the dressing room curtain tighter around the door. Goddess, don't let anyone see me. As a straight girl, I was not beautiful, I was "intelligent." I didn't look hot, I looked "serious." Lace was out of the question — femmes are belittled, thought to be weak, stupid, and forget it, honey, that isn't me. This is a dress I wouldn't even have thought of wearing when I was straight.

But now it's safe. My lover isn't going to think me incompetent if I dress a little femme-y, I think, fingering the strange layers hanging off my waist. Now it's possible to embrace . . . well, more of my . . . beauty. And this dress is the hidden side of me. I know this in the dressing room from the flush on my face. The dress's erotic power doesn't feel anything like the terrible memories I have of wearing skirts in the straight world. The air coming up my legs doesn't tell me that I'm exposed and unprotected in a world of men, but that in my safe world of sex with women I choose at this moment to make myself vulnerable to my lover.

The Dress

I don't remember taking the dress off: the next thing I know, I'm climbing back into my sweat pants and begging the woman, is she sure she wants to buy it? She is, and she does.

Then I'm striding across Valencia St. towards the gym to lift weights and practice my boxing. Only as a lesbian, I think: one minute covered in lace and nearly coming in a dressing room, the next minute charging down the street towards the punching bag.

On a folding chair in the women's locker room, staring at the tips of my high-tops and trying to calm my shaking hands, I'm amazed at how much I want this dress. I'm kicking myself for not insisting on buying it. I suppose if I hadn't been so struck with the dress's effect on me I would have argued with the woman or beat her to the cash register. Or maybe I was thinking, "this thing is so powerful, take it away from me, I don't want to deal with it." Or maybe, "this thing is so beautiful, I don't deserve it." Like a first kiss, no dress will ever be quite the same as this one. My hands are not a-quiver, or trembling even, I am out-and-out shaking with the way I felt in that dress. Naked. Powerful. Vulnerable. In fact, so vulnerable that I think perhaps the scenario would not be me, striding across the floor like a tough femme-top, but me, so raw, that I would arrive at this imaginary dance at my lover's side and hold onto her arm, both of us aroused by my exhibition.

I move into the gym to the big bag. I think about all that black lace. As I cover my knuckles, entwine my fingers with the wide Everlast fighters wraps, take a stance, pull one fist to my face, the other ready for the punch, I just shake my head and think, "Oooh, that dress."

WHY I HATE POETRY

WHY I HATE POETRY

I've got to tell you, I'm sorry, but I just hate poetry. I don't like the stuff at all.

Those neat little lines, stuck in the middle of a page, making you want more, and more. But there's never any more.

And so slow. Poetry is. Each. Line. Read sep-ar-ate-ly. Of wet. And woman. Moon to come and. Light. Of wet. Until I. Want to ask:

"Honey do you talk that way on the bus!"

There are some things you just can't describe in a poem. Like this woman's face. It's not a face like a jewel or a cluster of petals: you know in poetry how it isn't just a nice face, it's "the blossom of her soul" and she hasn't just got nice eyes, she's got "two openings to the galactic harmony" and such.

In poetry, everything is always something that it isn't. Orgasms are always waves and cunts are always flowers, of all things. In poetry, the nights are endless, the moon predominantly influential and the pain, oh the pain is just excruciating. Nothing is ever there for itself without something that the head thinks up, that the brain decides is the REAL definition. It's never just a pot on the stove and a cat in the yard. What a cluttered mess.

You just can't write a poem about this woman's face. It's a wonderful face, a worn face, hearty, with little lines under the eyes from laughing. It's all the color of a pecan. It's got a good nose and eyes that she can make look all big and dog-like or scrunched up and fierce like an eagle. Green eyes. Well, you can't say in a poem that after you were with her everything in the city was pecan and green pecan and green. And that after you touched her and her back was so strong and solid and her buttocks, well you just can't say what, except that she encircled you with those biceps until *she* was the feel of love: her big calloused hand — not just anybody's touch or some abstract caress — suddenly, when you thought of love you thought of *her* hand.

You know, for all the poems in the world there isn't a new way to say "I love you." After you've said it about a hundred times, and you've touched her cheek, you've mumbled it into her ear and her cunt and whispered it in public and screamed it when you come, you've still got "I love you" on your lips but nothing to say. So, you mutter, "here, I ah . . . brought you some flowers" or "didn't you say you liked bittersweet chocolate?" Or maybe just "Goodmorning."

And what about when you hear "I love you" and what you're longing for is "I trust you," "I respect you," or "I feel so safe, I'm letting you inside, I'm even going to let go for a while." When you start wondering about those words and where they went it's too much for words all straightjacketed into a neat little row. It's too much when you fight or fuck up when you swore that you wouldn't and you're both hurrying to work on your stuff and fix it all, quick before the other one leaves, like trying to patch the roof before the rains come and the sky is already grey. Well, then it's like "I love you"—a million reasons to say it but only one thing to say—"I'm sorry." Standing there, with your heart in your hands, like a little kid with nothing in the world and pee in her pants—"I'm sorry." I don't know. You just can't write a poem about *that*.

THE
CRY

THE CRY

The tears were still dripping off her lashes when she decided to make a cup of tea or get another box of Kleenex, maybe turn on the radio, but to definitely get a grip on it.

The tissues were collecting on the floor like origami ducks and she was lying deep into the comforter. It was decadent, indulgent, like watching an afternoon movie when there were dishes piled up. She had been crying for nearly two hours.

So Agatha pulled herself out of bed, slowly, untangling one of her long feet from the covers, nearly stumbling; she was slow and bleary eyed. Her best bathrobe: that's what she wanted. It was in the back of her closet and she pulled it on with slow, tender motions that pitied her arms. She hugged it around her belly. It was heavy and slinky, the way she felt about herself today and the satin-acetate was the color of her California pecan skin. The green lining even matched her eyes. She pulled the collar up around her ears and folded it under her chin. Peppermint tea, she thought, rubbing her eyes with her fists.

She grabbed her lotion from the bathroom on the way to the kitchen and picked up the kettle. She felt good, really, she thought, as she sat on a little stool to watch the water boil. She felt drained and raw and her skin tingled, warm from the inside. She smiled a little sheepishly. When she cried she felt like a child who could only hold onto something soft and let go of her head. She loved it.

Oh, let it cook by itself, Agatha thought, flapping her hand at the kettle. She got up and slouched into the living room, the tie of her bathrobe dragging across the carpet, the lotion forgotten in her pocket. I'll watch a movie.

Agatha flipped through the T.V. guide but couldn't find the right day, tossed the book down, picked up the lesbian newspaper. She wanted a movie. Bette Davis or Marlene, Kathryn. Well, someone who cried.

Like in the films, when the woman was tough and stood very still, turned on her waist, her chest tight and her breasts over to the left of her. She would show only her profile, "No, I'm not crying: you don't move me," but the tears would course down her face like a scratch.

Agatha paced in front of the television while the blue light brightened. She ran her thumbs between her belly and thigh, cradling the soft skin in her hands.

In the films, if they weren't icy ladies, they threw themselves into their tears. The woman would succumb and fall against someone's shoulder: Agatha could feel the woman's body crumpling against her side. "I can't bear it," the woman would say, and fall. Others would rush to her side, gather her up.

The Cry

Agatha eased herself into an overstuffed chair and remembered evenings as a child when she would lie in the dark, pretending to sleep. The hall light would snap on. Agatha would stiffen. Mother, the woman who ran everyone's show, strode down the hall. The little girl heard a voice strained and small, so unlike Mother's commanding, daytime tone. "Agatha?", the sound of a woman in pain, looking for comfort.

"Sweet baby, are you asleep?" she would plead and swing open the door in a dramatic gesture, silhouetted against the light that burst into the darkened room. In a loose robe that draped to the floor, Agatha's mother would stand there a moment: this was an entrance.

The little girl's heart would pound. She would sit up and reach out, as the woman came across the floor and crumpled into her arms. Agatha would strain her little body to hold her mother up.

"I'll take care of you, lean on me Momma."

It was exquisite. Exhilarating. Bette Davis in the arms of a 13 year old baby-dyke. Magnificent: being in control of the controller, her mother's warm skin next to hers, the smell of a woman wafting over the little girl. Oooh, cry Momma, cry, I'm right here.

Agatha got up and snapped the T.V. dial around. That was her family alright. Never a word about sex. A tacit agreement never to make any reference to it. But her mother and sisters cried with all the passion they could muster. Young Agatha could lie on the sofa in the darkened living room with the music playing, her forearm over her eyes, crying for hours. That kind of abandon was indulged.

Agatha scowled at the television game show. A woman with little barrettes in her hair was jumping up and down on high heels, lights flashing behind her.

Her mouth moved like she was screaming. She grabbed men and almost knocked them down to kiss them. No no, Agatha thought, a movie.

She set the dial to UHF. Mother's tears. At Christmas there was nearly a competition to see which child could make her cry. Mother would open her presents one by one: "Oh you shouldn't have," she'd say, and get a little stuffy-nosed. But then she'd open a special present, one particularly right: Agatha and her sisters never knew whose gift it would be. "Oh my goodness . . . Agatha."

She would stand up and turn it around in her hands, open it, close it; if it was cloth she would rub it against her cheek, the tears would well up, "my children love me so much," she would say and then she would cry for being happy and Agatha's Dad would grin a little indulgently and turn his head — women's things, you know. Agatha would hurt to see her cry and rejoice to see her tears. I must have done it right, I did it, I made her cry.

Agatha pulled one of her legs in and tucked her feet under her buttocks. Her eyes were puffy and her nose was thick. Her joints ached from lying curled on her side. She felt great.

The kettle started to whistle but as Agatha climbed out of the chair and headed for the kitchen, the doorbell rang.

"Who is it?" she called.

"Bettina. Hey I brought you those papers."

A collective member. Agatha closed her robe tighter around her, wondered if she had time to run for one that was not quite so femme-y, tried to get rid of her smile. Having someone at the door when she was crying was like getting caught masturbating or something: a pleasure she didn't want anyone to know about. She put on a mournful face.

"Sorry to disturb you," Bettina said, scanning Agatha's face and looking away. "But Joe-lynn said you wanted to see these flyers before the meeting tomorrow?" The woman was nervous. She didn't know quite what to say to a tear-stained face.

"Thanks. Yea." She could see the woman's discomfort, as if one of Agatha's breasts were hanging out or clots of blood were falling onto the floor.

"You wanna come in?"

"No. No thanks. I'm on my way back to work. Feel better, eh?" she said sadly. Bettina reached out and squeezed Agatha's arm, then turned and hurried down the stairs to the street. Agatha closed the door and grinned. Feel better? Well, maybe there's a sad movie on, she thought, amused, and turned to get the kettle.

SLEEPING DOGS

SLEEPING DOGS

A woman strides onstage in a 60's-style cocktail dress that is satiny and tight at the knees. She has on a coat and gloves. Her hair is teased and swept off her forehead. She takes off her gloves as she walks but then stops, startled by a man sleeping on a sofa. Only the man's shoes are visible to the audience. Though home only long enough for her to "check on the children" and take off one glove, her husband is asleep. She is crestfallen, then stiff and angry.

"The girls are sleeping . . . peacefully. John? John! For Chrissake," she hisses, realizing he is asleep, "I don't even have my gloves off yet!"

She turns in circles, scanning the empty room, at a loss, then looks him up and down and turns away in disgust, moving to a table where two highball glasses, a decanter and a yellow plastic ice bucket are neatly set.

"Well," she sighs, slapping down her gloves, "here we are again, just you and me" sizing up the emptiness as if it were a lover, "alone at last."

"It doesn't matter. It really doesn't matter, it was a lovely evening anyway," she says in the sofa's direction, "the music was wonderful and you know how I love to dance."

She turns to open the ice bucket and ceremoniously drops cubes into a glass with tongs, making as much noise as possible.

"This isn't disturbing you, is it dear?" she asks sarcastically and clinks the tongs on the glass. "No, of course not. And you're as responsive as ever. Well, I really had a lovely evening — Jack and his wife were there, did you see them, they were on the patio most of the night. I had a nice chat with Phyllis: it seems that business is getting better, though God only knows how. Those people are so slow and las-i-DAYsical," she slurs, "lack-si-daisy-cal" she repeats.

"You know, John, your wife was a hit at the party: I was witty, charming and there was a bevy of young men talking business with me — not that you noticed of course but it doesn't matter: Wendy's always telling me it's what I think that counts. And *I* think I was even attractive." She looks seductively at her husband. "John?" Her face falls and she turns to make another drink.

As she throws cubes into her glass, she lists the sins. "I'm gonna go watch the game, he says, and falls asleep sitting up. Oh Jeanette, I'm going to do some paperwork, I'll be right down, and then he's snoring in his goddamn chair. If I take you to the theater, I have to elbow you every few minutes. Do you know what it's like to be all dressed up, sitting next to a man who's snoring in public?

Sleeping Dogs

"If I hear one more crack about your BEAUTY sleep... .Oh God!" she snarls, "Here's to sleeping dogs." She drains her glass.

Jeanette stands with her hands resting on the table top, trying to regain a stiff, controlled composure. Each time a burst of emotion breaks through, she tightens up again, to act indifferent, regal, always like a lady. She is getting increasingly drunk, however, and her control slips more and more. She pours another drink.

"I hate sleep," she says, spitting out each word like a bitter seed. "It's such a waste of time. You just lie there, with your mouth open. I swear there's something wrong with wanting to sleep that much, with having a brain that isn't hungry enough to even stay awake.

"How can you DO it. You have no idea what it's like to not be able to sleep. It's like living in gel, I swear to you John. It isn't that I can't entertain myself," she says, quite drunk, "but how do you start a goddamn project at one in the morning?

"And what am I supposed to do at a time like this — a crossword puzzle? Huh? Oh I know, another load of your laundry, right — right.

"Everything seems so . . . inappropriate at this hour. I mean there are people sleeping, and one must be quiet when people are sleeping. Quiet until everything seems frozen, John, stuck to the tables and the floor--shhhh, mustn't wake them. I drag around all this dead weight at night — these people who aren't contributing but they're not gone, either. I'm never really alone, even when there's no one here.

"You know John, I'm almost afraid of beds. The last time Wendy was home, we were chatting in her room — you know how we are – and she was making her bed. Well, she reached over to turn back the blankets and my heart, I swear, it hit the floor. All I could think was — 'Please, don't leave me!! Don't go to sleep.' Really. That's when I realized that beds are my enemies.

"And you, you sleep through it all and then expect ME to make the bed in the morning — I prepare your means of escape."

Jeanette tries to re-gain her composure but she is very drunk at this point. Her arms flail when she moves them, a caricature of the lady she is attempting to be.

"Well," she says, as if to brush off the incident, "you fill my ice bucket and I make your bed. A wonderful marriage," she snorts and turns away. She sips, and stares off into the evening.

She mixes another drink.

"You know, John, I used to be so pure. The kids remember, I never smoked or drank much. I waited 'til all my girls were born before I touched any of it. I just got so tired of being good all the time. A gingham-check mommy.

"And now it's really the only thing that upsets you, isn't it? Crying doesn't work and getting angry — that gets me nowhere in a big hurry. But having a few in public — that makes you really uptight, doesn't it baby? Suddenly you can't pretend to have a perfect little wife and there's no way to sleep through it. Everybody starts to notice that Jeanette isn't happy.

"You know, I am really a wonderful woman," she says, crossing her arms and lowering her eyes as if to an opponent.

"I'm capable, I'm efficient — God, am I efficient, every step is preplanned. My employees know when they get an order from me, the job ticket's right there, the paper is waiting, the packing slips are ready and boy oh boy those shippers will be called before the job is finished — I bet you didn't know that, did you? You thought it was 'your system,' huh, your own 'business acumen' — my sweet ass, buddy. It's your wife, on top of everything. Not a move, without me. How do you think decisions get made? — the same way your goddamn socks get laid out in the morning. Your wife, John, *I* have the ability to command.

"Oh, tsssh, musn't be bitter. No no no no it's so unbecoming Jeanette, unflattering and . . . disloyal.

"But Marge, I say, I'm suffocating. You're my best friend. I can't breathe.

"'Oh Jeanette,' she says — you know the way she is" she says to the silent couch, "what am I doing, you're asleep.

"'Jeanette, she says, it's just because you have someone to clean your house for you — take an interest in your cooking again, honey, find a hobby.' Christ. I don't want a goddamn hobby, I want a lover," she clenches her fist.

"What an ass Marge is — as if I'd love you more if I cleaned up after you more. I can see it in the grocery store — 'Increase His Sex Drive Through Gourmet Cooking' . . . OH, I must run and get a garlic press, could you watch my basket for me'" Jeanette mimics, turning to an imaginary shopper beside her.

"I'm not a wife who bakes cookies, and drives to The Club in a little bitty sports car to sit on my little bitty fanny and sweat on a Tuesday afternoon. I am NOT a useless woman."

Jeanette stares into space for a moment, then turns back to her snoring husband. "John," she says pleadingly. "Oho John." He snores loudly, then chomps and slurps. She grimmaces.

"Christ, I think men are just put together wrong or something . . . though now I sound like Wendy. Did you know that the last time your daughter was home from college—for Gloria's wedding, I think it . . . yes . . . well, she said to me 'Oh MOTHER'—you know how she is—'it's very obvious that men just ROT faster.'

"I laughed. And then I said, 'Now dear, is that any way to talk about your future brother-in-law?' and she said 'Oh Screw, there are enough men in the world without letting them into the FAMILY.'

"I couldn't argue with her. There are . . . so many . . . men in the world. Rotting. But not fast enough—even though you do your best, don't you dear?

"Here's to sleeping dogs," she says, and drains her glass.

MARINA

MARINA

She's just too stoned, Elizabeth thought, looking at the woman whose head hung almost to the table. Elizabeth grinned, thinking the woman was an American college kid who had come to Amsterdam and, not believing her luck in finding legal hashish, had smoked herself into a stupor. Elizabeth had done it herself in this very bar. Joints would pass down the benches, pass the length of the bar on the other side of the room, be handed between select groups or by invitation only. Everyone in the place was young and everyone came to get high.

Elizabeth sat on a bench at the first of seven tables running the length of the room. Her black hair shone against the dark wood-grain of the walls and her fuschia tennis shoes were bright splashes against the wooden chair where they were propped. Piles of dog-eared magazines lay on the tables beside little puddles of tobacco, hash and papers. Elizabeth, a transplant from Manchester, in Amsterdam for over a year, usually smoked away a few afternoon hours with her single-skin joints kept for herself while she sat alone at a table, fending off conversations even in a public place. After all, she reasoned, there was really no point in talking to men and there weren't very many women out alone. Elizabeth pulled a paper out of the pack and opened a tiny zip-lock bag. Today, she questioned her own logic though: the silence had gotten so excessive that entire weekends could go by without her having spoken to anyone except the greengrocer and the waitress in the coffee bar.

She crumbled pieces of hash off a small block and pulled her tobacco from her coat pocket. The woman across from her had still not stirred. Her blood sugar's dropped too low, Elizabeth thought.

"Would you like some orange juice?" she asked, putting her hand on the woman's shoulder.

"Oh yes . . . I want some," she said with a German accent, as she lifted her head and slowly focused. "I have no money so . . . that would be nice."

"My name's Elizabeth."

"Marina."

The woman was a dark-haired German with a round face and clothes so loose Elizabeth could not see where belly joined hip or waist joined ribs. Marina wore pants and a long dress shirt, beads, a vest, and pendants around her neck. Yes, of course, Elizabeth thought, if she's not American, she must be German, looking like such a hippy. Elizabeth went to the bar to get the orange juice and returned. She rolled up her joint and lit a match.

"You stoned?"

"Stoned?" Marina repeated. She pushed a strand of wavy hair from her forehead. "No . . . I'm very sad you see. My boyfriend? He was just shot."

She looked Elizabeth in the eyes for the first time. "By the French police."

The smoke curled out of Elizabeth's half-opened mouth.

"What?"

"The police," Marina said, falling back into her seat. "We were in Marseille and they stopped us, for having long hair and no place to sleep. They took us to the station and my boyfriend? — he is French. Well, they checked on him you know?," she made the motions of a telephone and men scribbling notes. "He has skipped from the draft." Marina turned and her eyes seemed to lose their focus on the conversation to watch another scene far away.

"They wouldn't let me see him. They told me to go away, that they were going to keep him in jail." She laid her hands flat on the table and leaned forward. "He couldn't stand that. My boyfriend has not been away from me since he was 13. Truly. We ran away from home together. He couldn't leave me so he ran out of the station and they shot him."

"Good God," Elizabeth's breath was shallow in her chest.

"Right in front of me, they shot him. They are pigs, the French police, I tell you. Now he's in the prison hospital."

Elizabeth's joint burned untended in her fingers. She watched Marina with wide eyes. Her story had lifted the day off the ground and held it in suspension.

Marina mumbled to herself. "They won't even let me in to see him." She turned to Elizabeth. "We were on our way here and I didn't have anyplace else to go. Do you think he will mind that I couldn't stay?"

"I . . . I don't know," Elizabeth said, her brow creased between her eyes. How could she believe this woman, but how dare she not believe her. A part of her wanted to say, 'Oh, I see, nice chatting' and run all the way back to Manchester. Well, she had heard that the French police were brutal.

Elizabeth grabbed her forehead, at a loss, "do you have a place to stay?"

"For tonight. I only know one person in Amsterdam."

"Well, now you know two. Come on, I'll buy you something to eat."

"And some cigarettes?" The women stood up and regarded each other. Elizabeth smiled.

"Sure, some cigarettes."

Later that night, Elizabeth watched the tram pull away as it took Marina to a convent. The only 'person' Marina seemed to know were the sisters of a charitable order. Just eight hours between her and the streets, Elizabeth thought. The sisters will put her out in the morning. I would be worried if I were her, but in spite of it all, they had had a very nice evening. How could that be, she wondered?

Elizabeth had taken her to the women's bar, the Vrouwencafe. Marina had gobbled up the stew they served on Tuesday nights, sopped around the plate with bread. They sat at a small table on the balcony, at the railing, absently watching the clusters of women and the bartender pulling beers from the porcelain tap. With their legs stretched in front of them, they talked about the French police, demonstrations, tobacco, traveling with dogs, traveling with no money. Marina would talk intently about the world she saw and then, moments later, slump back into her chair. Elizabeth saw what she thought was the pain of loss and worry flood her, making her face go slack. Elizabeth would roll another cigarette, waiting. She thought Marina very brave and when her new friend focused on her face again, Elizabeth put her arm around the woman. They didn't know why they got on so well, so quickly. It was as if nothing else mattered but being able to put their feet up in each other's company.

Even though she went straight home after seeing Marina off, the morning came too early for Elizabeth. She had been sleeping heavily and she was late for work when she woke and threw on her clothes, crashed down the winding stairs of the apartment building and skidded across the wet cobblestones towards her bike, laying tangled in a mass of twenty others. She pedaled over the footbridges and along the canals to the cafe where she cooked, chastizing herself: breakfast rush was in 15 minutes and she didn't have any soup left from yesterday.

When Elizabeth arrived, she went through her routine in double-time. She stacked ten loaves of bread onto a shelf at exact arms length from her cooking station.

"Sorry I'm late" she muttered, still in her coat, half to herself, half to the manager who scowled at her from across the cafe. Tomatoes, onions, how much prep is there? The first customers had already come in and were waddling sideways between table and bench, shucking off their coats. Elizabeth strapped on her apron and then peeled off her coat. She had worked at the Egg Cream for six months. It was a small cafe on a back alley, a narrow room of wooden tables and low lights. The first floor of the building across the alley was the neighborhood bar, its heavy red curtains blowing in and out the door, even this early in the morning.

Marina, she thought, moving around the kitchen with a spatula and a knife. She'll be over soon. What can we do? Money. And food, well, maybe I'll do a bit of shopping before I see her tonight. A job is what we need to find her. Elizabeth chewed on the idea of Marina, puzzled on her situation, as she moved through her morning prep.

It had been a long time since there had been a "we" in Elizabeth's life, since she had taken care of anyone. Usually, she minded herself and followed the news: worked, ate, read the paper, went to sleep. The newspapers stacked up around her apartment, clippings hung from tacks all over her walls. She had a small tape-deck with a broken radio and no television. There was never activity in her apartment unless she created it, since no one visited and no one phoned. The women at work were chatty but distant, leaving Elizabeth to her long walks and her struggle against talking to herself, to her evenings of bathing, dressing, window shopping.

Today, Marina came through the door of the cafe, her hands deep into the pockets of a big wool coat, a rucksack over her shoulder. Elizabeth turned with a plate of food and saw her coming down the aisle between the tables. They kissed on their cheeks, touched shoulders roughly.

"Morning, luv."

"Hallo."

"Will you have some breakfast, I could sneak you a plate."

"Oh yes, certainly" Marina slid into a booth as Elizabeth returned to the kitchen. She made an omlette quickly, barely waiting for the green peppers to cook, buttered toast with sloppy strokes, dashed out and slid the plate under her friend's chin. Elizabeth settled into the benchacross from her.

"Ah, *danke*."

"Surely. So, how did you sleep. I mean, bad dreams?" Elizabeth asked tentatively.

"You mean about . . . my boyfriend?"

"Yes, I mean, have you thought about what to do?"

"There is nothing to be done, Elizabeth. I sent a letter to his mother today to say I am here. And now, I wait." Marina stared out the cafe windows. "Really though, I don't want to talk about him anymore. I just . . . wait."

"Yeah. O.K."

"But me," Marina said, brightening, "I slept like a log. Those beds they are so hard. Nuns, you know. Hey cook . . . "

Elizabeth watched the woman's face intently, waiting for the words.

". . . this is good."

Elizabeth smiled and leaned back in her chair.

"So, you know," Marina pointed her fork at her new friend, "I think I have a way to make money . . . good money."

"Oh?"

"I met some guy on the street, you know? He'll sell me speed. It's very easy to sell speed, Elizabeth, very easy. The soldiers love it."

"Drugs? Um . . . sells pretty fast?"

"Like cake," she said, luxuriating over the words, "like sweet German cake. You want to be partners? I have to . . . get money to start and you know, my friend, I give 100% interest. Elizabeth you give me 60 *guildens* today, I give you 120 *guildens* tomorrow night."

Elizabeth looked around the restaurant. Drugs. Well, it did seem the most sensible way for Marina to get money — the best money is always dirty money.

"Sixty *guildens*?"

"I leave everything I have with you. I buy the shit and sell it and that night? I come to your place. To give you your money and get my things. What do you say, you have 60 *guildens*? I make it 120, plus there is 60 *guildens* for me so . . we make the same profit and you get back what you put in — a wonderful business."

Elizabeth transferred some of her day's wages from the cash drawer into her apron and from there to Marina. The two women drank coffee until another order came in for Elizabeth. Marina would come to the house that night to transfer the money and collect the knapsack and jacket she left as collateral.

That evening, Elizabeth walked around her one room apartment, straightening the piles of papers. It was a tiny place and things needed to stay neat for there to be any feeling of air, even with tall French windows the entire length of the room. Elizabeth opened them to clanging church bells and a pale sky that seemed thinner for being below sea level.

She set the table with two glasses and a bottle of Dutch gin, the hashish, tobacco and a basket of fruit. She was picking over the apples when the door buzzed. The latch was at the top of the twisted stairs and she yanked on a cord that snaked along the railing to swing the door open.

"It is Marina."

The German strode into the flat and emptied her pockets, littering the table with blue and orange Dutch money. The women hooted and laughed as they flattened the bills and calculated: 120 for Elizabeth and a 60 *guilden* profit for Marina. They pulled out their chairs with mischievous grins and settled down. Someone to rub elbows with, Elizabeth thought, her eyes big and bright like a child being served her favorite food, a woman on the edge of her seat waiting for the first morsel of tenderness. Elizabeth opened the bottle; Marina turned the tape player around and around in her palms and slid in a tape.

Marina

Despite the two pots of tea that followed the gin, the women were asleep by 10:30. Marina was curled on the sofa. Elizabeth was stretched languidly across her foam pad. She slept more heavily than usual, deeper into her chest so that in the morning, she came out of sleep quite slowly. We can go out to breakfast together, she thought, and rolled onto her side, grinning. I'll buy her coffee at The Golden Bough.

But when Elizabeth opened her eyes and focused on the couch, Marina wasn't there. Elizabeth listened for the toilet, then sat up. So where was she . . . had she gone?

It was very early, the light in the room was still grey and the curtains drifted across the floor on a light breeze. She said she liked me, 'it was a pleasure' she had said, so where was she? Elizabeth's eyes roamed over the window sill, the piles of papers, the big table laden with the previous night. She pulled herself slowly out of bed. There was the bottle of gin but where were the stacks of money they had counted and re-counted, piling them in checkerboards, piling them in stars, scrambling them up and laughing? Two dirty glasses and an empty bottle of gin. But no money. And no friend. Elizabeth smarted like a child whose buddies have splashed her with mud. The table was so barren. And where was the tape-player? Elizabeth's stomach tightened. Marina had acted like a confidant.

She looked around her flat, considering the morning as if looking into an empty bag. With her hands on the table and her nightshirt hanging from her shoulders in the same limp gesture, Elizabeth wondered what would have driven the woman to theft. Then she remembered the fading eyes and the way Marina slumped in her seat. Elizabeth had looked at a junkie but not seen her.

She went to her bureau and pulled on a pair of pants and t-shirt, laced up her tennis shoes and, grabbing a little money from the back of the drawer, tore down the stairs to the street. Halfway to the main thoroughfare, she couldn't remember if she had locked her door but she didn't care, she had to be out of the house, away from the empty table. She could see the woman's face in front of her, remembered her clothes on the chair. Marina had found a better place for her pot of mums and it was Marina who had told her about the cheese store she had seen on the *Linbensgracht*.

It didn't matter about the tape deck or even the cash, what hurt was that now Marina would work at staying away. Elizabeth could phone the convent Marina first stayed in—maybe she had gone back. Maybe I'll drop into the bar after shopping; she couldn't have gone that far away. It doesn't matter about the money—they could work it out.

She went to the greengrocer by rote and made her decisions in half her usual time. She bought two pounds of potatoes and two of carrots and enough green vegetables for four meals. Even though she went to the outdoor stall every two days, she bought two cartons of milk, two bottles of juice and a whole pound of butter. Her purchases covered the table top at the cash drawer and were a tight fit in two large bags. Elizabeth circled her arms around the sacks and lifted them off the counter.

Striding up the cobblestones, she tried hard not to think about anything, until the weight in her arms finally cleared her head. Of course it matters, Elizabeth thought, suddenly losing her steam. You can't have someone in your house who steals from you . . . and lies, as well, for all she knew. But she was headed in the direction of the bar to start searching for her anyway. She had bought the fixings for the dinner she was going to prepare for Marina; she had gotten extra milk and butter for her friend, just as she had decided to do yesterday.

Elizabeth slowed her stride. She had to buy these groceries, even though Marina wasn't there. The woman set the two big bags onto the cobblestones. The food would rot without Marina — Elizabeth would never eat it all alone. Elizabeth looked at the extra large broccoli and wedge of cheese she had bought for their dinner. She should leave the bags in the street, she thought, just to be relieved of it all, anything, anything other than cooking for two, yet dining alone.

A SHIRT WITH NO SEAMS

A SHIRT WITH NO SEAMS

Driving through a mountain pass, the woman concentrates on the wintery road, the way it winds, the banks of snow, the dark patches that may be trouble or the brightness that may be ice. Reflected lights in the rear-view mirror throw a streak of silver across her eyes and I am taken by the subtlety of the colors — grey of hair and moonlight and dark eyes, soft skin.

Tonight, like never before, I see a butch side of her in the determined uplift of her chin and the sure, peaceful lips. I want to touch her and to really feel something but somehow her beauty goes into me and doesn't seem to stay.

I am like a shirt with no seams: all here, certainly, but open and unraveled and in bad need of mending — not just to close a little hole that lets the warmth leak out a bit — my sides are rent apart. Feelings blow through me and leave me vacant. My lover's gone, our love is over, it's the end of an era.

And now, as a woman hanging open from her shoulders, I realize that feelings grow in small enclosures, where warmth can build on itself. It's impossible to warm a space that's open to the winds.

I hadn't realized that it took faith to love, but I can see that now, as I watch the plans of the grey woman fall through my torn pockets. I had plans once, grand plans, trinkets meant something and matching earrings and my shirt in her closet, but I lost the woman and the plans are just a joke now and my faith in believing is unraveled to the hem. I guess a cynic never feels anticipation, since it takes so much hope to build excitement.

I live like a rag woman, draped through with the past. The phantom of the woman I loved comes to cackle through all the arguments we never finished, no matter where I am or who I'm talking to. She reminds me of "our house" and "our love" and that I'm always in the wrong place — it should be *her* jacket I hang up in the evening and her coffee I pour in the morning.

Tonight, driving with the grey-girl and wanting to love her, I see that my first job is as a seamstress, to be a woman sitting patiently, meticulously re-piecing herself with tiny stitches, working against my fear that the stitches will break again. I can't see the future and I'm not even sure what shape I am making but I at least can believe in the mending, stitch after stitch.

MORNING GIRLS

MORNING GIRLS

"Everybody keeps telling me 'that's pretty heavy for a 12 year old' but they don't know—I got muscles," Eliza said, closing one side of the newspaper over the other and sliding it into her canvas bag. She sat on the stoop, looking up at a woman running in place, her knees bouncing up to the level of Eliza's head.

"Whata ya doin'?"

"Jogging," Pamela said sheepishly, her hair flopping on her forehead.

"Can't you stop?"

"You're not supposed to," but Pamela shrugged her shoulders and sat beside Eliza on the cold cement steps. "It's for your heart, see, and you need to keep at it or you don't really work yourself. When you get to red lights and street corners you're supposed to run in place."

"I get it. What's your name.?"

"Pamela. Pamela Torgin. I live right across the square. That yellow house over there, that's it. So what's your name?"

"My name is Sam." Yeah, that's it, Eliza thought, goes with my muscles.

"Nice name," Pamela grinned. Eliza grimaced. "Well, I mean it suits you."

"You wanna see my muscles?" Eliza wasn't sure why she was being so friendly. She didn't show her muscles right off to just anyone but this lady seemed alright. She wasn't too fussy; she knew she looked stupid running in place and her hair was all sticking out in directions. At least she wasn't one of those prissy kinds whose jogging suits never got dirty. Shit.

"I got 45 houses on this route, except on Sundays and then I got 52, well, plus the Church — that's 53 and on Sundays this bag is even heavier. Sometimes when they put in a lot of advertisers — that's what they call all that . . . "

"Yeah, advertisers . . . "

" — I hate advertisers. They fall out all over the place and on rainy days? — well, they slide out from under my poncho. Sometimes my Mom's on the phone to somebody before I even get home, you know, some lady who's just got to have her California Living Magazine. Then I got to walk all the way back, way up there, almost to Portrero Hill. Sometimes I try to get my sisters to go and my brother — he's so lazy he won't even drive me." to

"Sounds like hard work."

"Yep."

"Must be about 5.30."

"You think? Yeah. It was 5:15 when I left the house."

Eliza was usually silent in the mornings, just watching the few pedestrians out this early. today, she leaned closer to the woman, conspiratorially.

"I'm in a girl gang."

"Yeah? What kind of gang."

"We're not real nice."

"Great. Nice is so boring."

"There's five of us, except when Bethy can't come because of her mother but we're real close. We have a special place we meet and we go all over the neighborhood.

"Couple of weeks ago—we glued the mailboxes shut at the Lutheran Church. And before that we soaped the windows at the Catechism class. You know, they make all the girls wear dresses, all the time. That's why we don't like them. And McClintock's place—we hit it all the time. You know, we never get caught. Nobody ever suspects us. Well, sometimes somebody will see us and start screaming—'stop those boys', or 'hey sonny, you get back here'—but we just laugh. Nobody can catch us. Bethy's super fast and I can climb fences 'cause my arms are so strong.

"Look how dirty my hands get from this. My Mom tells me I'm not supposed to touch anything but how are you suppose to work not usin' your hands, huh? I tell you, on collection day, my right pocket and all up here,—ink."

"Well, it's part of the business. I guess your mother will just have to accept it."

"Yeah, she's alright, my Mom. We're going to be together forever, you know."

"You and your Mom?"

"No, me and the gang, Bethy and me and Carrie Ann and Sue. We signed papers and buried them and we're never giving each other up and none of us would ever tell any of the secrets. Ever."

"That's great. I wish I had a gang like that. Me and Bethy, Carrie-Ann and Sue, forever. Yeah, that sounds pretty nice." Carrie-Ann

"We can run faster than anybody. Really. Every year we win at Field Day—all four of us."

"How long you been delivering papers, Sam?"

"Two years. I'm strong, look" she said and clambered off the steps, dropping the heavy canvas bag and the roll she had just made. "Look." She pushed up her sleeves. Eliza grimmaced, steadied her shoulders and flexed. Pamela smiled at the skinny brown arms in the morning light, a tiny bulge rounding her bicep.

"Pretty good, huh? I'm going to play softball next year and I always get picked first cause I run so fast. Well, Bethy's a lot faster."

"Sam, you're a regular athlete. And speaking of which, I should run. It's getting late." She slapped her hands on her knees and pushed herself off the step. Pamela bent and stretched, making faces of protest.

"How come you do it if you don't like it?"

Pamela ran in place. "Because it feels so good afterwards. Hey, nice talkin' to you Sam," she said, her knees bobbing like a cartoon horse.

"Yeah, maybe I'll see you again, I'm here every morning." "Yeah,

Well, that made sense, Eliza supposed, doing something because it felt so good afterwards. It was like getting up in the morning. Her mother would wake her and then climb back into her own bed and Eliza would moan and groan but this, being outside, was always worth it. She looked at the willows, the dew on the grass. Being out so early in the morning

Morning Girls

when there was nobody else around was like an adventure.

Like being with the gang. No one else knew where she was or what she was thinking. No one else ever saw this light. It was like sneaking. She would stroll along her route, singing songs to herself, talking to Bethy and Carrie-Ann as if they were there. She was captain of the gang because she spent the early morning thinking of schemes for them. And they thought it was 'cause she was smart.

But the best part of the morning was always coming home again. She'd strip off her clothes and sometimes she hid them so that no one even knew what she had looked like. She would kick her shoes under the chair by the window and climb back into bed beside her sister, who wouldn't stir or even notice she had gone. Eliza would lie on her side, in the warm bed, surrounded by the smell of her sister, and grin.

Well, that was it, the whole bag together. One day this thing is going to rip and then I'll really be in a jam, she thought, hoisting it up and slinging the strap over her shoulder. Eliza headed down the street, tossing three papers fluidly onto the top steps of the three adjoining walk-ups. She shrugged her shoulders and picked up her pace.

So, about the gang, she thought, slamming the ball of her fist into the glove of her palm. What the hell can we do? We've got three hours between the end of the paper route and the beginning of school. Let's see. Spray-painting the Armory's no fun anymore, we already did that and besides, Mission Street is too busy. And we don't want to hit the school because then we have to stare at it for days and try to not look guilty. I don't know, she thought.

Eliza turned the corner. Here's my favorite house. The Morgan's had one of those little Pekinese dogs and it slept right against the porch door, rain or shine. And ever since she knew it was there, Eliza went out of her way to aim carefully and hit the porch door square in the middle. This morning, she loaded her arm up, cited down the ridge of the paper and BAM hit the door with a whack. Well, the dog jumped off its little pillow like it had been shot out of the center of the newspaper, straight out into the air, stiff-legged and landed on the cement. It leaped onto the plastic sofa with the cabbage roses and ran along its back cushions BARK BARK BARK YAK YAK YAK more like a parrot than a dog and onto the end table, pressing its nose against the screen.

Mrs. Morgan, an early riser, came out onto the porch, just like every morning. "Now Muffy", she said, and picked up the little thing, its legs on either side of her arm kicking and pumping to get at Eliza. The older woman closed her house dress with her free hand, flung the latch and stepped outside for her paper. her

"Thank you son," she said, just like every morning, with the little dog going YAK YAK YAK on her forearm.

Eliza would just sort of salute and stroll down the sidewalk never quite sure why the woman could hear the dog but not the thud of the paper.

Alright, the gang, Eliza thought, trying to wipe the grin off her face. What can we do? Can't be tormenting little dogs, now what's in store for us? I prefer cats anyway, she thought, especially ones that don't have women to take care of them. Eliza remembered the stray cats she had seen in the junkyard near Army Street. And what about all those cats out at Land's End? They never have anyone to pet them or bring them nice food in a little dish. They sure don't sleep on a little pillow like that stupid dog.

Bethy likes cats — sometimes she's silly about it, like that time we were running from McClintock's and she's climbing over this fence to get away and sees a kitten on top of a garage and just has to stop all the action to rescue this little thing. Eliza smiled, remembering how Bethy made her crawl on top of this pickety fence to get on a garage that was already leaning, about to drop from being rotten and beat-up.

"Are you sure this shed can hold me?" Eliza whispered, frantic and a bit annoyed at having to be the hero.

"Get the kitty, 'Liza, she's cold, can't you hear her."

"If she scratches me, I'm droppin' her in the mud."

"Sshh, they'll hear you."

That's it. We'll get us some milk and bicycle like hell out to Land's End — there's millions of cats out there. Bethy will love it. She'll think it's the greatest idea of the year, I just know it. 'Course maybe we'll be late for school but shit, it's not the first time. Milk. She had been wanting to get the dairy for a long time — now that was a challenge.

She'd climb the fence, on the side where they kept the garbage bins and take a couple cartons from the stacks in the back so the drivers couldn't see right away when they got in. And she'd pitch them over the fence to Carrie Ann, who . . . yeah, she could catch them in her bike basket 'cause hers was wicker attached with leather straps. She'd love it — pretend it was outfield practice. Eliza liked the idea of pitching the skinny white cartons high into the air, the stakes being a tell-tale puddle if her arm got wild. And then they'd have to peddle like bats out to Lands End.

But the best part of the whole plan was the sight of Bethy, cliffside, the wind blowing her blonde hair like a movie, with all the kittens circling around her legs and her cheeks pink and all happy from such a crazy way to be around cats.

I'll tell them at school today and we'll do it tomorrow morning. They'll love it. A hell of a way to spend a morning.

Pamela ran around the park, chuckling to herself. What a baby dyke that kid is. In a few years she'll be loving the morning for my reasons, she thought, remembering the woman sleeping in her bed.

Sure, the light was soft and the birds out, there was even fog settled on the soccer field this morning, but after the first five minutes of her run, when she established her pace, Pamela thought about sex. Lap after lap, running 'til her legs burned, she plotted the seduction of Sandra, lying unawares under a crumpled down quilt.

The woman had no idea that Pamela ran for erotic reasons: she thought she was into health — and she was, but she was also devoted to her morning strategy sessions. Today she sprinted up a small hill, steadied her pace and cruised behind the pump station, bright with graffiti. The first of the cross-bay buses were pulling out from the garage. She'll be lying on her belly and this morning, well, I'll start with the basics, she thought, the lips in her mind kissing Sandra's ankles.

Sandra would flinch and pull away. Pamela would grab her ankles and pull her towards her.

"Baby," Sandra would laugh sleepily. "Baby stop," grabbing for her disappearing pillow. Pamela, her body slick with sweat from her run, would move up over the woman's buttocks and back and lie full length on Sandra's warmth.

"Morning," she'd murmur and nestle her face in Sandra's ear. She'd slip her hands under her lover's ribcage until, Sandra, arching forward, offered breasts that were crumpled and warm with sleep.

Pamela ran the straight-away beside a line of eucalyptus trees. She would press Sandra's breasts into the woman's chest and part her fingers for the nipple. Moving in circles, she would knead and hold the nipples until she saw a reaction near Sandra's eyes, pinching, then releasing, to turn her lover onto her back. eyes,

Pamela stretched her arms out and increased her pace. She could feel the tired muscles from her push-ups of the day before. She liked the idea of throwing off her clothes and climbing under the comforter from the bottom up. She liked the idea of holding a reluctant ankle with one hand and with her palm against Sandra's cunt, knibbling and kissing the long expanse of fleshy calves and thighs.

Sandra struggling against her grip, that pleased Pamela, and she thought perhaps she wouldn't say a word and wouldn't let Sandra see her, but would slowly push Sandra's legs apart until she was spread to her limit and then lick and bite her legs in circles and lines of pleasure, her pumped-up arms and wakeful hands strong against the woman's protests.

"Ah woman, you're . . ." Sandra would murmur against her pleasure and her sleep, but Pamela would only move forward, to blow warm breath against her cunt and slide her nose into the slit of her body, nostrils gliding along the rippled folds. She would gently part Sandra's lips and curl her fingers into her black hair, pulling her labia up and open, kneeding them down to expose the clit.

Pamela ran through the eucalyptus grove unaware of the trees. She thought of how her mouth would come down slowly, how she would moisten her lips and pour wetness to shield Sandra's clit against the tongue that would sit for just a moment before it circled and began to vibrate. She thought of how Sandra would moan and roll her shoulders to press her face into the pillow, tangling her black hair. Sandra's cunt would wet the woman's face as she lifted her hips and ground herself across Pamela's chin, humping the mouth that shook back and forth, the tongue that teased her hole by tapping then darting inside then tapping, to slide up to her clitoris again.

This morning, running, Pamela realized she had increased her speed considerably and that her fists were clenched at her side. She shook them out and in a burst of energy, tore across the dewy soccer field. But the turf was water-laden and when the wet started oozing into her shoes, she turned back to the asphalt track, laughing with the way Sandra had carried her out of the morning. She wiped the sweat from her forehead into her hair with the sleeve of her t-shirt.

Pamela ran the curving path between the children's swings and slides. Perhaps she would try a different tactic. Maybe this morning she would take her clothes off outside the bedroom door, slip in without a sound, and climb onto the bed, straddling Sandra's head. With her cunt just above her lover's face, Pamela would part her own labia.

"Kiss me goodmorning, baby," she would say. She knew her cunt would widen from the noise Sandra would make. She would lower herself to the woman's lips and then pull herself away, just out of reach, as her lover woke and strained forward.

"See how sweaty I am from my run," Pamela would say, caressing her own thighs, stroking her hands upward into her cunt and wiping the wetness across her lover's cheeks. "I'm drenched, baby."

Pamela ran behind the pump station again. Perhaps she would sit on Sandra's face and let her float between the half-sleep of sex and the bliss of half-sleep.

Or maybe she would hold herself aloof and, reaching behind to grasp the woman's nipples, tease and play and pull until she felt like muffling the woman's cries with her cunt.

Now which would it be, Pamela wondered, as she pounded through the eucalyptus trees. She looked at her watch. A full 30 minutes of running. Her heart was pounding and her lungs felt full. She could see her nipples through her soaked t-shirt and her legs were burning. She looked across the park at the Bay Bridge and Oakland in fog, the morning being gentle even to the shipyard. Plan A or Plan B, she wondered with a smirk, as she tore down the steps and headed home. Either way, it was a morning well begun.

GLORIA

GLORIA

A woman sits on a folding chair, in plaid wool pants, a white shirt with a Peter-Pan collar and a tiny pearl brooch. Banners of The Twelve Steps and Twelve Traditions hang behind her, a coffee urn sits beside a plate of little cookies.

She raises her hand, looks furtively around her when she feels she's been called on, points to herself and shifts in her seat.

"Um, hello" she says nervously, "my name's Gloria."

A chorus of voices responds "Hello Gloria."

"I've never spoken at these meetings before. It's . . . well, all of a sudden, very frightening, like if I open my mouth it will just keep spilling out. I guess I just wanted to thank you all in the program because, well, I went home for the holidays and you know, it was really different. I've been waiting for things to change for years and finally, things are a little bit different.

"My mother's an alcoholic but even before she started drinking the family was full of the whole scenery of denial, you know? My mother would rant and rave and we would just stare out the window or look at our dinner plates, all of us thinking, Oh God, she's at it again.

"And like you said," Gloria points to a woman several rows in front of her "the family is governed by the member with the worst temper—well, Mother ran everything. She's one of those powerhouses from the 50s who ran her family like a theater company or something. Probably because she couldn't have a theater company, but anyway . . . the rest of us avoided her temper by living in outer space.

"When I was 17 I was a hippie and I had this badge that said 'Lost In Space'—you know, after the T.V. show. I thought it was really funny—like I'm high, don't expect me to do anything—but it wasn't funny because I really had no safe place except my head.

"I swear that's why I'm a botanist now—I just have to be grounded in the earth, like I'm chanting 'You don't live in the sky Gloria, you don't live in the sky.' I feel safer when there's pete moss under my fingernails.

"When I left home, I finally realized—my God, I'm a survivor who knows nothing about taking care of herself. Because when you live around someone with such a changeable temper you don't initiate things for yourself—you never know how they're going to be received. When there's a commander in the room, you follow commands.

"I guess being a 'co' is sort of like being a servant. It's 'go ahead, throw a tantram, I'm right here to pick up after you.' When I was about 16 I remember my parents coming home really late from being on the town and my mother was loaded. They were fighting before they were even out of the car and my mother came pounding up the stairs screaming 'I demand you make love to your wife — do you hear me? I DEMAND you make love to me.' So, my father disappears into the spare bedroom or something and I've been awakened from a dead sleep and I'm flipped out. Well, I come tearing out of my room — mother's little helper you know — because I can hear her crying by this time and she's standing on the stairs looking at her dress and she goes 'Christ I *hate* menopause. Look at me, I'm *scarlet*.' The blood is pouring out of her and running down her legs — she's mid-step, it must have started just that instant — and she looks like she's been electrified."

Gloria is silent for a moment, looking into her empty styrofoam cup.

"So, I take her by the elbow," she says, in a softer voice, "and lead her up to the bathroom and . . . I get down on my hands and knees on the cold floor to strip the girdle off this woman because it really *is* scarlet. She's swaying back and forth and I'm yanking on her — it was really difficult — and I look up at her and say, 'Mom, you're really drunk.'

"Well, that's all it takes and she goes off — 'Oh, you think you're so superior,' she says. My God, the woman's sprawled across the sink with her dress hiked up around her waist and she's looking down at me, screaming, 'You're *nothing*, you shithead, nothing!'

"Well, she climbs into bed and I'm standing there rinsing the blood out of her clothes at 4 in the morning, thinking 'someday she'll know how great I am.'"

Gloria turns in her seat and falls silent.

"Well, I'm in this program because, let me tell you, I'm tired of waiting for 'Someday.'

"It's to the point where I can't hardly bring myself to do anything nice for myself. I drive this ratty old Volkswagon and somehow I feel safer in it than if I had a new car, you know what I mean, better rolling death than confront the feeling that . . . well, that I *deserve* good things in my life. I'm trying, though, I'm re-decorating and I've been shopping for carpet, but I tell you, it's torment. I come home and collapse — am I worth $8 a square yard or only $6.50 a square yard.

"I mean I'm not trying to make it sound like everything is my mother's fault — that was really important to me about this program — that it's not about blame. You know, my old man was a drunk for years and then one day he sobered up and ever since then the family's always thought how strong and resourceful he is, but I'll tell you, when I was home for the holidays I finally saw — thanks to this program — that he had just turned in the bottle for the power of the 'co' — oh he Lords it over my mother. And I swear that's why he quit — so that when he started screaming and trashing her she couldn't say 'hey, you're a fuckin' alc, too.'"

Gloria covers her mouth with her hand, feeling that her emotions are getting away from her.

"It's as if he's dependent on her alcoholism for his power. God, it was really a shock to see *his* sickness, not just hers.

"Not that I let on or anything — that's always been one of my hardest things — showing emotion in public. And anger is the hardest emotion for me. You know as I listen week after week I see that our common pattern is one of powerlessness, regardless of how we act it out. Who was it last week — oh Cheryl, right—who said that you have to feel powerful to feel angry, to say 'this is right and this is wrong,' or 'hey, I have some dignity and you're violating it.' Oh God, that's almost . . . impossible for me. With women I love anyway—getting angry at men in the world is no problem, but women I love . . it's like the angrier I get, the more I fall over myself trying to eliminate her responsibility for it. I've had some of the sickest relationships . . . with some of the neatest women, you know? I talk about, well 'WE need to change this.'"

'I'm so obsessed with being good company . . . because angry people like my mother were such a 'problem', so disruptive and they look foolish. I felt so oppressed by her anger because there was no way to get around it so . . . well, maybe I'm trying to be extra good company to make up for her. Or something, I don't know.

"Now, my sister's reaction was totally different. She was Fury Incarnate, screaming all the time. And then, a couple of months ago, she called me—she's in Al-Anon in Los Angeles—and she told me that she realized that as long as she kept screaming at Mother she could blame everything in her life on Mom and she would never have to be responsible for her own life—her anger was avoidance.

"God, it's so complicated. Well, I just wanted to share that tonight because no matter how confused I get I know that this is the one place in town I can come and say 'Hi, my name is Gloria and I feel like shit.' So, thank you . . . all."

Gloria turns, a voice says "My name is Martha."

"Hello Martha," the crowd says.

"Last week something happened that reminded me how much I appreciate these meetings . . . "

THE SUCCUBUS

THE SUCCUBUS

She timed her arrival to the corner well: without breaking her stride, Margarite stepped into the bus as the last passenger entered, dropped in exact change and slid into a seat alone.

There should be no reason for feeling flustered, she thought, a bit confused. Her clothes were clean and well-pressed, her hair combed in place. Even her briefcase was tidy and she was well prepared for the meeting she had called.

I'm not really flustered, she puzzled, but something felt amiss, like remnants of a bad dream that delays my breakfast, makes me forget where I've put the jam, or something. Silly really. Margarite smoothed the collar of her tucked white shirt and its thin black bow.

There was . . . it was . . . wait, her forearm told her, it was her breast. There was a burning, in her breast, like a mouth on her nipple and (she shifted in her seat) now a pinching feeling, was it . . . teeth on her nipple? No, of course not. Margarite looked down at her blouse, then glanced to the side (was anyone looking?) Could anyone see her hardening nipple and she swore there was a tongue running 'round and 'round its crumpled skin.

Margarite cleared her throat, straightened the crease in her slacks and pulled her briefcase in front of her. Absurd, she thought, the flush growing in her cheeks, I'm on the 8 Market towards Sansome St., just like every morning.

But she swore there was a mouth on her breast, circling her nipple, taking bites.

The bus lurched to a stop and Margarite braced herself with a hand on the seat in front, left it there to shield the excited breast. Maybe if she read the paper, she thought, but she didn't want to take her hand down. A woman with a large parcel edged past her seat, a young girl in tow. Businessmen, oblivious to everyone, pushed down the isle. People were standing up now, holding the railings, their bellies at eye-level, so Margarite stared straight ahead. She couldn't move, pressed against the seat by the busy lips inside her blouse. Her breathing deepened. She was pinned, trapped by the suck, suck, bite.

I am NOT a prisoner, she thought, I am Margarite LeCarr, I am going to work like any morning. I slept alone last night, in pajames, and I do NOT have . . . lips on my nipples. The idea was absurd; never mind the feeling, the thought of it was preposterous. I'll read some papers for the meeting – mind over matter, she thought, and set down the briefcase between her legs and yanked out a folder. Ah, she could move from the back of the seat. Margarite smiled. It must have just been . . . my bloods or something.

The Succubus

But the woman didn't get the folder opened before the tongue flattened and covered her entire breast with wetness, wiggling a tongue point into the crease between breast and chest. Margarite gasped, looked sideways. Her breast was being lifted up, sucked. She could feel the spittle running down her mound onto her belly. She could see it, she could, the surface of her left breast higher than the right, being held and now kneaded and squeezed. Margarite cleared her throat and pulled up her collar.

"Excuse me," Margarite said, as she gathered her things to her chest and scurried out of her seat. The woman beside her looked puzzled. Margarite pushed through the crowd, gasping and whining as her nipple was twisted. "Pardon . . . me . . ah . . oh, excuse Aah, coming through . . . BACK DOOR!"

"Goodmorning Mr. Taylor" she said as she stepped into the wood and chrome elevator.

"Goodmorning Ms. LeCarr."

"Margarite."

"Tom. Hello Harold," Margarite tried to steady herself. She turned. "Vivian, goodmorning dear."

Up the floors and out the doors, the workers held their attache cases and their styrofoam coffee, raincoats over their arms, a higher class of knit suits remaining as the numbers climbed. a

In her office, Margarite set her briefcase down as if the journey had taken months. What was going on with her body? At 43, her hair was graying and crow's feet cut in towards her deep-set eyes. She had a round belly and wide thighs, long fingers, a regal carriage. But this morning she felt like a girl, confused by her first blood.

Margarite poured herself coffee. Diane, her assistant, was already in: the phones were on hold and Margarite could hear the file drawers rolling back and forth. She ran her finger across her manila files but wandered aimlessly into the front office.

"Goodmorning dear," she said softly.

"Goodmorning Marge," Diane said with a grin, spunky, looking up from the folders to study the woman's face. Diane was 35, with hair as thick as a dog's and a nose that drew a viewer up its arching smoothness to her eyes. Constantly moving, Diane always looked like she'd just gotten off the racket-ball court, no matter what she wore. There was always the tell-tale pink in her cheeks.

The two women knew each other's lines and wrinkles, they knew what puffy eyes in the morning meant. Diane had listened to many stories of Karen leaving Margarite and moving East and she had been gentle during those months of pain when Margarite stared out the windows and cried during lunch.

"I forgot our breakfast," Margarite said softly, "I'm sorry, falling down on my job."

"Well, those blintzes are a hard act to follow," Diane said, flashing brown eyes and giving her friend an out. When Margarite didn't take the bait, Diane scanned her face closer. "Bad dreams?" didn't

"No," Margarite said hesitantly, averting her eyes. She wasn't sure what was happening. How could she explain this, even to Diane, her only confidant.

"Well," Diane said, shoving the file drawer closed, "no time for breakfast anyway, only twenty minutes before this fucking meeting."

"Right," Margarite said, and returned to her office, where she opened her curtains to the sun and plopped into her high-backed chair. Her coffee sat steaming on the file cabinet in the other room while she stared out at the willow trees, their tendrils langorously streaming in the breeze. They dipped and skittered across the morning.

This was not her imagination, she reasoned. And nothing unusual had happened to precipitate it. The night before she had not dreamed, she had not touched herself or slept naked. She had lain motionless — the perfectly smooth and tucked sheets told her — for eight hours and thirty minutes, the same celibate night she had lived for the 9 months since Karen had left her for a new job and a new woman on the East Coast. Her body was something that sat behind her desk, sat at a cafe table, lay cold under sheets at night. It was better this way, easier. cold

Sex wasn't even something she thought about, except occasionally when she was in a crowd of lesbians and she found herself imagining things — her hand against a woman's cheek while she stood talking about business, or the shape of the breasts on a woman across the room, or her hand slipping across the small of a woman's back, embracing, touching, kissing anyone in range. It happened rarely. She was just more controlled than that.

But this . . . this attention, well it was wrong, it was bizarre. Next time she would have to be sure it didn't show. Margarite turned her chair from the window. Next time? she asked herself, you're planning on it? Margarite remembered the feeling of her breast being lifted and a flush rose through her body. of

Now, what was this feeling . . . no, not again, she thought and smoothed the front of her blouse. No, it was not her breasts, but there was a tingling . . . in her legs. Margarite sat back in her chair. Like the touch of a feather tipped with down, the sensation ran up her ankles to her calves and played behind her knees, bringing her blood up inch by inch. Suddenly, it teased the curve of her hipbone and drew across the top of her thigh. Her mouth opened and her eyes glazed over. It stroked the side of her neck; she laid her head back and gave her temples to it. To what, she thought, to whom?

It brushed her lip; she shivered and turned away, the feather proceeded and the willows outside draped themselves through the air like a dozen soft boas. The feather took her back and forth, rhythmically, in long sweeps up the front of her body, then down her shoulders and across her buttocks, as if she were not sitting, as if she were not clothed, not on the 12th floor with things to do.

Margarite swayed in her chair, eyes closed, the muscles of her neck standing out, red from ears to chin, little beads of sweat gathering under her nostrils. She allowed herself to be lulled into the rhythm.

Just then, her tormentor switched from feather's down to quill tip, and dug into her shoulder. The pain burned her skin. Diane walked into the room with Margarite's coffee cup. The quill scraped from shoulder to base of the spine.

"Margarite, you left your . . . "

Margarite shuddered. As she grimaced, the phantom plunged fingers into her cunt, up where it was wet from her bus ride. The pain drained hot from her shoulder to her vulva, giving her a bigger hole and a throb like a drum. She slammed her hands on the table. hole

"Ahh, I'm not well," Margarite stammered, "I mean I . . ." she watched Diane take inventory of her flushed face and unfocused eyes. Oh not HERE, Margarite pleaded silently. What am I saying? Not anywhere, leave me alone.

"I need to go home," she said, pleading.

"Home? You? But the meeting!" Diane replied, confused, shocked. "Home?

"Oh yes. Well . . . you can handle it. Yes," Margarite said, brightening. "That will be fine. We've been over the proposals a number of times, Diane. You helped write them. It's a fine opportunity for the board to see . . . "

"Margarite," Diane said, warning.

". . . to see how valuable you are. How capable. It's a wonderful idea," she said, standing up and searching for her papers. "Really Diane, this can't be helped" she said, not quite certain what she meant.

"Is it your stomach?" Diane asked.

"No."

"The flu? Your joints feel alright? Margarite you're a wreck. You don't look sick you look absolutely frazzled."

The two women stood silently while Margarite packed her briefcase, hoping it at least resembled the papers she brought in this morning, trying to lay out the proper folders for the meeting. The stalemate continued, a tight silence in the office, until Margarite picked up her report and handed it across the desk.

"Here, you'll need this."

"Oh god." Diane paced the width of the room, exasperated. "Alright . . . I'll call you a cab."

Margarite sat back in the taxi, her beige linen coat draping on the seat, her legs crossed at the ankles. The cab plunged up Market Street, the reverse of the route she had just taken. This is the first time, that I have ever, she thought, taken a day off work for . . . nothing . . . for sex. Margarite was incredulous. In how many years of being sexual, she thought, and why now? And how could she be expecting to . . . and so didn't that mean that she was an accomplice and so making love with . . . this . . . phantom, this . . . succubus. love

Yes that's what it is, a succubus, a woman spirit who comes to seduce in a woman's sleep. She had read about them in reference to the saints. A nun locked in a convent cell and denied the world, except a view of the herb garden from her barred window, would be visited at night by the spirits of women.

The succubus came when the nun had spent the day watching the bent backs of the novices in the fields, torn by the sight of women so far away, as her pen and ink and scriptures sat idle. The nun would go to bed early, slipping under her coarse cotton sheet, still in her hairshirt. She would toss and turn. A touch would come to her, her temperature rise, 'No, no I mustn't' she would murmur but turn her buttocks to the moon. The succubus would laugh and hovering above the length of her body, set her mouth on the nun's ass.

In the morning, the nun, her eyes sunken from lack of sleep, her hair wild, would be found in the corner of her cell by the novices who brought her breakfast. Gripping the window sill, her neck covered with black and blue bites, black and blue shoulders and forearms, the nun would grit her teeth against her words and the novices, prohibited from stepping inside the threshold, would stare open-mouthed at the woman's bare legs and cold toes. would

"Sr. Angelina! Do you . . . require anything?"

The taxi that took Margarite home pulled smoothly into the drive. She sat very still in the back.

"Scuse me?"

"Yes? . . . oh, of course, how much do I . . . oh, I see, $4.50," Margarite fumbled in her briefcase. "Keep the change," she leaned forward with the money and caught a glimpse of herself in the rear-view mirror, her neck purple with bites. She dropped the bill onto the front seat and pulled up her collar, her breath caught in the chest.

"Ah, Miss, it's a bit short here. That's $5.50."

"Oh. Yes. Excuse me, let me give you two. Thanks again," she said weakly and slid out of the door. She opened the collar of her coat and pulled on her clothes, seeing just what she expected — black and blue marks all over her shoulders. As the taxi drove away, she stood clutching her lapels. What I see, I am, she thought, and what I think, I feel. Oh Goddess, this is very dangerous.

Margarite stood in the drive looking up at the second floor of the peach Victorian where her curtains slowly blew in and out of the open windows. It had been years since she had seen her tiny front lawn in the daylight of a working day. She opened the front door and climbed the polished stairs to her apartment. Everything was the same as she had left it: the plants at the top of the stairs, the French doors open to the front living room, pillows just so on the green velvet sofa, armchairs, fireplace, candlesticks, closed and polished writing desk — it was all the same, but so peaceful that Margarite felt she was disturbing something. She looked at the light on the polished floors, the way the flowers looked in the afternoon, everything in the room a different color than she saw in the evening. She set her briefcase down on the sofa, hung her coat up, her short heels clacking on the floor. She turned back to her living room. She felt like an intruder.

Margarite moved to the china cabinet by the fireplace and lifted down a tumbler, opened another cabinet for the Scotch and strode into the kitchen for ice.

Back in the living room, Margarite kicked off her shoes and plopped into an armchair, set her feet on a square footrest. I guess I must work like my mother, she thought. Four years without a single break.

Her mother would come home tired and disgruntled and ease herself into her overstuffed chair with lace doileys on the arms. Mrs. LeCarr would fold her coat over the arm, pry her shoes off with her stockinged toes and sigh.

"Gite, baby" she cooed to the young Margarite, waiting by the television, "come rub Mother's feet, please baby, I work so hard."

Margarite would turn on the television and hurry to pull up the ottoman. This was the finest part of the day. Mother worked sooo hard, she deserved attention and Margarite was happy to give it to her. The little girl scanned the t.v. guide every afternoon: what would Mother like? She prepared the woman's special chair, polished her table. And when Mrs. LeCarr finally came home, the little girl would hold back, expectantly, waiting for her favorite phrase, "Gite, baby, come rub Momma's feet, please baby." Flushed and silent, Margarite would hurry across the room, sit on the flowered ottoman at the woman's side and grasp one of her ankles. She would kneed and rub and hold the foot like a breakable object, like a lamp to rub to make wishes come true.

"Momma?"

"Yes, pet," the woman sighed, stroking her daughter's head but never moving her eyes from the set.

"I can't do a good job through these stockings."

"What dear? Oh, well, alright. You can take them off Gite." The two had a special ritual. Mrs. LeCarr would remain totally still as Gite slid her little hand under the tight A-line skirt to her garter belt. Or the woman would slowly pull her skirt up to expose the clasp, one side at a time. The little girl's eyes took in every inch. Gite was so gentle, the soft warm thigh making her hands tingle. She grasped the black garter with both hands. Gite's body was hot everywhere, her nose overcome with the smell of her mother. She slid the sheer stocking down the thighs, dragging her little fingers along the flesh, over the knee, across the calf and off. Gite let it accordian fold onto the floor. Mrs. LeCarr leaned on her other buttocks to receive her daughter on the other side.

Now, with her hands on flesh, Gite would massage with a new vigor, rolling the soft skin between her thumb and finger, stroking the calves, pushing into the arches, pouring all the energy, the expectation of the afternoon, into her mother's skin. "I work so hard," her mother would say, "I deserve my . . ." whatever it was at the time: her Sunday sleep, her fancy food. Work made it right and for Gite, hard work made this skin and touch and caress, made these woman-smells possible; hard work meant Gite's hand slipping into the tight, hot space between the hem and the panty leg.

Today, in her own apartment, forty-three and ill at ease, Margarite sat forward in her seat. You do NOT fantasize about your mother, she thought. Margarite glanced at the bruises on her shoulders and, setting her Scotch glass on her knee, felt her shoulder blades for the beginning of the scratch. You've never touched your mother above the knees and you better not start thinking about it now, Goddamn it. Margarite leaned her head against the chairback and closed her eyes.

"Momma, I can't do a good job through these panties," she murmured. 'Alright dear, you can take them off.' Let me sit between your legs, you work so hard, let me nuzzle inside your folds, let me bite your thighs Momma. I want to see your head against your chair, I want spit sitting in the creases of your lips, give me your titties again, different this time. My mouth on your cunt, my lips teasing your lips, fingers pulling your hair, Mother, spread your legs further, that's right, touch my ears with your thighs, I'm eating you. Yes, yes, drape me back across the ottoman, my pigtails on the rug, I know the tops of these thighs Mother, to slip my hand around the back to your buttocks one hand in back one hand in front, a little girl wiggling into your cunt, I dive again, my fingers plunging in while I eat you Mother, my little girl's fist sucked back up where it belongs, fucking you Mother, you scream for ME at night.

Margarite opened her eyes. Wide. She was . . . good Goddess, she breathed, she was draped backwards across the ottoman, the afternoon sun striping her belly and legs in her executive clothes. The Scotch glass was spilled on the floor. The smell of a woman was heavy in the air. Margarite clambered up off the floor with difficulty. Her hand . . . was wet. Viscous come clung to the webs of her fingers, curled into a fist.

It can't be, she thought, turning in a circle, scanning the room for a woman she knew she wouldn't find. The succubus was in control, could make her fantasies more real than she had ever wanted. Tears well up in Margarite's eyes. I do not cry, she thought, but look at me, she turned to the mirror. I don't have sex, but I've been fucked on a bus, in a cab, in my office. I'm covered with bites and bruises and scratches and, she eyed her hand with suspicion, I fuck. She wasn't really in control anymore. She knew that now. Even though she felt she was totally in charge of herself, her cunt had always broadcast her need to her constantly, feeling so swollen and insistent it was as if it walked a few inches in front of her. Now Margarite knew that she had never been in control of her body — she had consistently denied its needs but had never controlled its desire and now the succubus had taken away even her ability to deny herself. She was being fucked and, she smelled her hand, she was fucking. Truly now, she was what she thought and she felt what she saw.

THE SHARDA STORIES

THE SHARDA STORIES

Sharda stood at the gate, her rubber boots ankle deep in the clear, wet snow, the spring snow, crystaline, and heavy with water. It was that immovable snow on the brink of melting that capped the posts and made it easier to climb the fence than open the gate through it. Snow so warm it was colder to the touch than the icy snow of blizzard. Sharda lifted the stuff off the post, scraped at it until it was a bowl and set it right-side up onto the post again.

'Should take me three hours to get this box to the post office,' she thought. 'Back before dinner.'

Sharda jumped over the fence, and hauled up a box bound with string and tape and red-wax seals. She walked towards the barn, snow pushing against her ankles.

The barn had a ring around itself where the ground showed through. It seemed a bit sunken. Water poured through the eaves from a slab of snow that had moved from the peak and was being shaved, little by little by the sun.

'I can go behind the barn where it's deepest, out to the cattails and over the creek, make it there and back before the storm,' Sharda thought, looking at a fattening line of grey in the sky, fluffed and rising over the hills, shimmering silver above the lake, then drizzling when it reached the flatland.

The storm, she said to herself. But it wasn't the storm Sharda was trying to beat, it was the dusk. It was the four- to six-time of day when the peach, then mauve, then electric blue light threw new shadows in the house, a new pressure on her chest, if the day were being squeezed into the ground.

Sharda would come home from work at dusk with a hunger in her chest: everything must be in order. She would throw things into place, still in the pace of the work-day and the freeway, focused intently on work, more and more frantic as the minutes passed, as if something were being stolen from her. She hurried to prevent the theft.

There had to be something, a pleasure, an accomplishment, an event to make her feel that not the entire day had been spent for someone else. There was something they couldn't take from her — this that she did for herself, hurry get to it before they take it all, she would whisper as she paced, 'before your evening is only preparation for tomorrow's giving, the morning's work.' Sharda would stalk through the house looking for it, her palms itching for it. What is it tonight? Reading another chapter, dancing, where is it tonight?

To give up the rest of the day, Sharda thought. All these late night women who can't let go of the day. You see us in the bars, wondering, 'is there something more?' Give me more, an insatiable feed me, feed me, night give me a little more up the lip. Bring on the night and the shadows. Bring on the rock. The woman near the light in her leather jacket, talking long distance, bring her here. Make us grey around the creases, give us bit of shade around the round part, eh? Pencil us in, a little darker on those late nights alone with no time. No shape to time at all: the shadows seem to push out the walls for more breathing space.

This morning, Sharda had been hesitant to awaken. Trying to keep her eyes closed and feel the length of clean linen down her legs to her toes, pulling the ragged blankets up around her neck, she tried to warm herself back into dream. Today. Would she find work, or boredom? Or just formless hours that she longed for when she had scheduled ones and which she sliced away with little rituals of cleaning and letters until time was in a more manageable size and she could finally sit down at the typewriter to work at herstory. That's all errands are, she thought suddenly cross, scruffing at the snow with the rounded tip of her boot and moving the box from her hip to her shoulder, a way to pare down time in a soothing way. Can't become overwhelmed by potential. Sharda, she scolded, so stubborn and so sure.

Sharda reached the second hill and listened to the wind raking the stubble. She tossed the box into the air. It landed on its edge and settled. She pushed her hands into her pockets, pulled her arms close to her chest and, watching the clouds rushing towards the flatland, thought of the soft white paper at her desk and the story of the Mediterranean dancer. Of Ashata. Parcel out time, Sharda thought, prune it and tease it with cups of tea and lamps just so, take yourself to the past and back again, like stepping boat to pier, boat to pier. Just enough of a dose of today to keep your balance.

The Sharda Stories

Ashata strode into the courtyard with belligerence, the slit edge of her white wrap flaring out at her thigh.

"Ah, curse these women and their constant industry," she muttered as she held her fine belly and leaned against the wall, one cheek against the cool wall, one cheek to the hot sun.

Ashata squinted against the brightness and through her lashes saw blurry, golden women in colored waist-wraps and beads that caught the sun. They crouched over big bowls of seeds and pods, breaking and grinding and sifting, three to a bowl and two behind, packing gourds, their motions hazy from the rippling heat. They poured seeds into flat baskets with hot coals and tossed them to sear the chaff. The grain would sit in globular baskets under the long table, or in the huge round storage basket of thick branches, the one sitting outside the ring of houses, on stilts.

Maya was sitting under the trees with her stick, telling tales to the young girls sprawled in the yellow dust, fingering their new tattoos and rings that marked their ceremonies, pouring dust through their fingers onto their thighs, braiding their hair, watching the insects as they listened to the herstory of the women, with their mouths open as if to suck the words from the old woman.

"Seeds and pods," Ashata murmured, "seeds and pods." She would prefer to be running with the cats, over the hills, flying above the stones with the sleek cat a pace in front of her legs, the wind pushing the short black curls off her forehead and tugging at the string lasso bag in ready at her waist.

To bag birds with the cats. For this, she would strip herself down, take off her ceremonial rings, the anklets that told of her trades among her women, naked except for the tattoos that told of her lineage and the gold paint of her own sweat.

Ashata thought there was nothing finer than to run until there was no more sensation of running. To run into the sun when she couldn't see the ground, to run until the air seemed to pour through her body as through a hollow gourd. To tend her cats and predict their success and try to smell the bird at the same moment as the cat so that, still running, she and the silver grey cat would jump into the air and, at the same moment, bring the bird down.

But there had been no running for three moonfests now. Ashata could not find any way to improve her nets and the feathers for gifts and rituals were nearly gone. Her cats had taken to sleeping in the sun and listening to Maya's stories, while Ashata ground flour until she could taste it through her lungs.

Only a little longer, she thought, and they will be old enough to be hunted again.

Tonight, she thought with a start, tonight is the ceremony. I am given the end house. I leave the youngers' for one of my own and we will burn fire in the night and wash the walls with rosemary oil and I can dance. Ashata opened her eyes and saw the elders conferring on the storage of the seeds and flour. The children had been sent into rest before the night's festivities.

I can dance tonight and everyone will see what a fine belly I have, Ashata thought.

That night, the elder women joined behind the end-hut and carried torches to the fire circle where the youngers clustered excitedly. Ashata sat alone in her best waist-wrap, lonely and trembling, then proud and wistful, catching the occasional glances of the others.

Maya began the chanting for good fortune while the elders circled the group again and again, finally stopping to place hands, first on Ashata's head for peace, then her shoulders for strength, her breasts for love. She stood and joined the procession to the end-house. She went inside and sat in the middle of the floor. Slowly, she rose, took off her waist-wrap and hung it across the door frame so that the light of the torches glowed through the fabric. She stepped outside and all the women, with the youngers, ran back to the fire circle and passed the bowl of mushrooms.

To dance, Ashata murmured, chewing on the mushroom, to dance and dance. The drums began. Slowly. To reach every woman, to pound on every belly. Ashata felt it growing in her, knowing that the women would make the rhythm more and more complex, as if to say, 'Ashata, you vain beloved, try to run over *this* terrain.'

Ashata began to dance, scuffing the soft dust, the firelight glimmering in her brown eyes, glinting off her nose-ring, her earrings, muted on her fine, olive skin. She began to dance. She began to whirl, shaking her curls and dipping her head, her finest multi-colored waist-wrap out like a saucer. She danced until her feet were a blur to the children, her knees bouncing up, the parts of her body each with a separate rhythm, each frenzied, fast, she whirled and whirled. To dance and dance the fire a blur, spinning so fast the fire seemed to be on all sides of her, a hundred fires. She felt lighted and asleep.

The elders stood in unison. They had seen Ashata's soul fly out her crimson mouth. The women began wailing. But Ashata continued to whirl, as if entranced. The youngers on the drums laughed — they had done it; a terrain of the drums so difficult the sure-footed Ashata had lost her soul. They had seen it rush over their heads to the hills where she hunted birds.

The elders grabbed the children and leafy boughs and ran quickly towards the hills. They ran past the granary, waving the boughs to scrape the soul out of the sky. They ran with all their strength, since Ashata's soul was very fast, having lived in such strong legs. They ran chanting to cajole the spirit back.

It hovered around their heads. They circled it and, with their branches, brought it down into the vessel made of their circled legs with the small children between. Closer and closer they gathered, pushing their hands inward and downward, crouching around the panting children.

"Close your mouths," a woman admonished, "this is Ashata's soul, not yours."

An elder drew a small gourd of honey from a pocket in her wrap and placed it in the circle. The women drew closer and closer until the spirit leapt into the honey and the woman covered it with her hands. The elders began to laugh.

In the village circle, Ashata lay twitching in the yellow dust under the buttocks of a friend. The women gathered around her and stroked her face. They pushed on her temples and slowly poured the honey down her throat.

Sharda set the box into the snow and flexed her back. Lost in her thoughts, she had completely forgotten the lay of the land and the snow. She had been walking without a sense of being there, transporting herself to her old cement bedroom in London, to the kitchen of a former love and back again.

It gave her a faith in getting older, these experiences layered upon each other so that each moment was there for itself and brought with it re-enactments of moments from the past. Life had no chronology. It came back to her like snapshots, helter skelter. Her memory brought her a vision from her 23rd year, then her 12th, then her 24th, her 25th, her 16th. For Sharda, a memory was not a practical tool, it was a method of transport through time. Exact moments could be duplicated to the smell and wet of the air, the feel of cloth on her shoulder, breakfast in her mouth. Sharda saw things as a conglomeration of isolated moments. As soon as something was realized it became so deep a part of her that the journey to the lesson was obliterated, the small events leading to those moments were forgotten.

Years ago she worried about losing the images. She hoarded shells and stones, pulled up flowers, took photos to capture sights and keep them forever. But the shell she stuffed in her pocket without seeing broke on the way to the house, the grasses looked only that color against the sand, the light could not be reproduced, the fire could not be sketched. Soon, each time she bent to snatch, she stopped.

So why be an historian, Sharda thought with a grin, amused at catching her own inconsistency. Perhaps to put the past in exact order? To guard against the loss of little slips of time? Well, herstory was certainly needed, she thought. Men immortalize the immaterial—the battles, the parchments of their own pompous achievements, leaving untold the greater flow of time and culture. And women's herstory is always written in conjunction with men's. We have no time-line that charts our culture as a separate people, which is what we surely are. It makes our view of ourselves so distorted, she thought.

Or maybe I am an historian to give chronology to a longer span of time than my own short life, to people my past with even more women: my own life, my past lives and the distant past of women. All these women, she thought, the ones carrying baskets on the road, the Medieval guild workers, women on horseback, all their beautiful faces, all these women.

The two women in black came thundering across the frozen marsh, mud flying out from the hooves of their horses. The first woman spurred her mare ahead several paces, then reined it in abruptly, jumping down from its back before it had stopped.

"Never!" she shouted and twisted the reins in her closed fist.

The younger nun dismounted with caution, frightened by the violence of the Abbess and her agitated horse. The last Council had pushed the older woman to fury. After years of battling them, the bishops had gained enough power to annex the convents, to turn the world upside down and put the dependent monasteries in charge of the very convents that had ruled them for centuries. For forty years the Abbess had controlled one of the largest double monasteries in Europe, teaching the monks and fighting to maintain the autonomy of her nuns. This morning, the

Bishop and his entourage had arrived in full regalia to publicly remove the Abbess from her position and install a young monk in her place. Rumor had it that by 1125 the Rule of Enclosure would shut all the nuns in Europe within the convent walls, forever.

"Never!", the Abbess hissed at the frozen ground, pacing up and down with her black skirt kicking out in front of her. "After centuries of peaceful, just management, is this what is to become of us — copying their books and mending their frocks? We, who have taught them everything! After this constant struggle to keep them from stealing our manuscripts, from degrading our good works and our erudition?"

"Surely the Rule of St. Benedict . . ." the younger woman ventured.

"Ack," the Abbess spat, "the Rule? Men have no rule but the constancy of their own greed."

The Abbess turned, then looked gently at the trembling woman. "Twenty-five years together, Marie," the Abbess said, using the old name of her lover. "We shall see no more young women — oh, don't think I don't know. These young ones don't run towards service to Our Mother and the poor, they flee the yoke of marriage. And so what have we to offer them now? We are the only schools left for women — are we to copy books that we wrote ourselves, now under the name of a man? Forty, fifty years imprisoned within walls we have built, never to see a lay-woman, a child, a village? Marie, it is a very evil hour. Even the Queen, who has fought so long with us, is powerless. Marie, we're to be imprisoned . . . all of us."

The history books on Sharda's desk hinted at things, gave her tendrils of facts with which to weave her pictures of women of the past.

"Women heading households in the 1700s were brave women, because in that century, at the height of the persecutions, it was women living alone or in communities of women who were most often accused of witchcraft."

The Sharda Stories

The stout woman stood legs spread at the top of the hill, her eyes fixed huge and black on the smoke rising above the village in the distance. She ground at the seeds in the mortar and pestle with the anger that showed in her face.

"We are next," she muttered. The clergy was one day's ride away and they were burning, woman by woman, until there would be no one left who remembered the reign of the mothers.

"A species of thieves and murderers. Bounty hunters. Twenty-one shillings a'piece to them. But not us. Not the women of my clan, we'll not submit to their collars of spikes, to their racks and spears and boiling oil, to turning daughter against mother."

She, with the pestle in the mortar, grinding at the poison.

"Tonight we join the mothers of the sea. Push the paste to the top of our mouths and walk off the cliff hand in hand." She chanted the ancient curse of the Furies:

"Oho ye young Gods, since ye have trod under foot the laws of old and ancient powers purloined,
Then we, dishonoured, deadly in displeasure, shall spread poison foul through the land,
With damp contagion of rage malignant,
Bleak and barren, blasting, withering up the earth,
Mildew on bud and birth abortive.
Oh Venomous pestilence shall sweep this country with infectious death."

That thick, black smoke. It stung her eyes from miles away, it clung to the insides of her nostrils. It will sit in women's lungs forever, she thought. She shuddered. She spat. She ground at the seeds with hatred.

Her mind could see them coming, a long column of rigid-back men, like mutants, riding towards the village with their white banners of sterility flapping in the morning wind. Their most useless, their most powerful at the head, in cloaks and badges and pompous symbols to show who could oppress the most. She could see the greed in their eyes.

It was her own death to see them riding across her fields, tramping through her beds of herbs. All her life she had been stalked by them, heard reports of their murders miles away. A woman would come into their village and tell the elders late at night: she heard their wailing in her sleep.

"Mother, what is happening in the square?" she had asked when she was eight and had ridden to town for the market. "Why don't we sell our medicines?"

"Keep walking, child. Hold your head up, keep silent and keeping walking. They've hung the apothecary and her sisters," her mother whispered when they joined the others. "Hitch the horses."

Ride away, leave the village, all the women together riding miles from their home to this spot at the edge of the sea to begin again. Women joined them late at night and in the morning no one spoke of where they had come from; these women had no past.

"Now the clergy is here." The woman looked across the hills to the black smoke rising. The men of death have pushed the women of life to the edge, have made us choose death. But *our* death. She was glad she wouldn't be there to see them. But she knew what they would do. The men would ride into the village and steal the books of medicine first, then turn to the women and ask:

"And so what do you know of the devil?"

The woman would stand with her feet firmly planted. she would stare at him from under her eyelids.

"The devil?" she would ask. "The devil is a man."

Sharda balanced the box on her shoulder and fingered the twine around its middle. She knew these hills well. Her feet knew the rise and fall of them, the knoll to the left, the nestling dip she had just passed, the covelette. Each of the spots brought echoes. It seemed to Sharda that the women's breath still hung in the trees from an outing last month, that that bird on that especially bright afternoon had just flown by.

She straightened her back, lifted her chin to the breeze and felt the clumps of practical concerns and plans falls away, shed off her clothing like the clumps of mud off a sheep's belly. She felt the nervous tingling that usually hovered on the inside of her skin begin to drain inward, pouring back into the center, solidifying, calming.

The box held straighter on her shoulder, the weight settled on her hips. She strode forward concentrating on the cold air pressing on her face. To walk

The Sharda Stories

until there was only the sensation of moving forward, conscious of the foot that lifts. Moves. Sets. To be conscious of the foot, the locus of all organs, the nerves, and so the sentiments. The foot, and the box.

BOX ONE. Sharda thought of packing boxes. Of moving on, of waking at 3 dreaming that your clothes are flying through the air, saying goodbye to her (but she's my lover, I love her and I'm standing here stuffing things into boxes) when she isn't there wishing you didn't have to leave (the things could stay on the shelf) packing away the arguments sealing conversations that never finished things in brown boxes can I store them, back in a month moving again how will we ever find you brown boxes it's so much easier, you quip, you make a circle of friends and when they disappear one by one you're free to pack and leave, to watch the scenery with your feet on packing boxes. The small one of chocolate wrapped in paper you take to the basement of the Spanish post office, to tie and seal with red wax. The ones you hold on your lap in the bus, moving, one by one. The presents in newspapers in boxes. The scraps in the bottom. The ones you throw down the stairwell after being so tender that's it goodbye to the old life, the junk's on the living room floor.

BOX 2. Deep behind the rain forest, the wide place where the elephants roam as they will, back behind this, an old woman lived in a very large cement building. This morning, she was bent over three packing boxes, mumbling and writing down the contents on a fraying brown clipboard.

"Two, mumm. Lookin' good now after a wash," she said with a brogue.

She stood straight and flexed her back, limber and softening, at that point in her aging where the skin goes buttery and a woman's frame is more truly her own, settled in, still holding up all the changes. She tucked the clipboard tight under her arm and wiped her hands across the backthighs of her baggy pants, lifted her foot to check the strap on the tai chi slipper ('must get me glasses checked') and scribbled 'glasses. check.' on the pad in her hip pocket.

In her smock were lists of last week's errands and contents of her vegetable bin and who sent Solstice cards last year. Bits of paper with the expiration dates of her tins of peas and a chart with their order on the shelf, scraps listing garbage pick-up dates and when the soap was bought, who had phoned last May and the numbers of shoe repair shops, the order of the books under the bed and all their past due dates, the birthdays of her ex-lovers, the lineage of her cats, which birds appeared at which windows when and whether the elephants always passed her house on the full moon, which was her latest inquiry, having carefully recorded their movements every night for years, penned their migrations into a fat book where she sometimes wrote little lists in the margins.

The books she held under her arm were her favorites. They were paginated lists of the contents of all the packing boxes in her attic. People for years had been bringing her bits and pieces of sets, the end of the lot and ones of a dozen. She would clean and sort and pack. To number and chronicle and file in a huge room upstairs that was the length of her very long building.

"Ah, the heart of a librarian 'n the mind of an engineer," she said today. "You're a dangerous one."

In the attic, the floor shown between the boxes, then dulled as the clouds passed between the sun and the woman's skylights. Boxes were grouped in threes and sixes, eight in a cluster and one to the side, Champale boxes with small yellow tags, brown boxes with blobs of sealing wax, wine boxes with smooth cursive writing along the side, crates bound up with string, all with huge black numbers written with a fat brush. Pathways snaked across the room.

Crumble. Born Arabella Crumble, she renamed herself Jay. She scratched the spikes of her silver hair and looked down to the windows. Lists. To list all the lists. The books of lists were clutched by their tabs and make-shift handles. The books of lists of the contents of boxes. Of file drawers. Of shelves. Jay clutched her lists and grinned, thought about the two electric blue boxes in a clearing of their own.

'A' **Blue Box**: Jay stood in front of the blue box, her fabriced toes touching the glowing blue paper, pulsating electric blue paper, thin and easy to crinkle. She had had a time constructing this box. The top was never sealed and rarely folded flat. It was filled with photos and empty frames. Jay frequently came to stare.

In the picture, two women are in an Arboretum, the Conservatory, a building like a glassy insect, a dragonfly. They stand in the Conservatory, surrounded by orchids and white-washed walls, a fat plant in a wire basket hanging above them. Its thick leaves are succulent, twisted, the roots of it are bushy nodules of moss. The woman is reaching out to touch the other woman's cheek.

Jay picked up another old wooden frame. Three women sit around a rectangular table in an old print shop, posters of orchids on the wall. They drink coffee. Three dykes with ink on their hands. The marble stone, the wooden type cabinet, the black platen press is behind them. One's feet are on the table, one's foot is on her seat, one sits on the back of an old leather chair.

In the round frame, a pale English woman is on a grey beach, her arms akimbo, legs bare. She wears a huge white Aran sweater, sleeves to her finger tips, round shoulders to her biceps, the hem at her thighs. She is talking to her goat, a black and white. Her goat is very small and feisty and the two are being very animated in the way you let yourself be with an animal. The woman looked up, and was caught showing a huge grin.

'B' Blue Box: Most days, Jay chose not to open the other box. It was usually sealed. Today she lifted the lid and stepped back several paces. She never looked at the photo closely: it seemed to have a grey mist over it.

In the photo, the steps are long and shallow, like a tier almost, running the length of the church and then some. The cool cement slabs in Venice never let you see the ground, the foundation of a church makes it an island. Faye sat on the steps with her knees up, feeling the cold stone against her buttocks. She had ridden a train that had sped out from the mainland across land so narrow it disappeared from the sides of the windows. The train seemed to the skimming above the water.

At the end of the church steps where she sat today, the water was flat and black until the next group of buildings, curving around them into lagoons and canals. The church's doors were open, draped with damp, old velvet. The dank air pressed against Faye's back, smelling like the air from a crypt, like the air from a building that had been flooded, then drained a month later. The air poured from the church's doors deathly wet and older than anything she had ever smelled. She put her head on her knees.

Yesterday Faye had received a letter telling her that Rebecca had cancer again, this time in her lungs. Faye had stared at the page, then folded it precisely on its creases and slid it gently into the envelope again, hiding it until she could think about it at a better time, open herself to the feeling when she was more secure, as if needing a day to build supports around a door that must be opened.

Today she lay her head on her knees. 'I mourn the loss, goddess, her body.' Faye rocked back and forth, back and forth. 'I mourn. The loss.' She felt Bec's silky, naked body crouch behind her and sit straddling her on the cold cement, this phantom Beca with her baby fine hair against Faye's cheek, the two women pressed tightly.

Faye could feel an icy spot on her lover's body, a blue lung, this icy rectangle where Bec's lung should be, burning cold through Faye's back. Around them was the dank smell of the church. Faye looked over the water and saw a bending figure, a woman honing a plank of wood with a long lathe, making a coffin for her lover, pushing out the pain with the strokes, bent over this box as her way of protecting the woman, even in the ground.

Sharda would nearly be coming up to the farthest fence and the old pine. She slung the box onto her other shoulder and slapped her hand against her thigh. The pine tree was where she came to sing and she could feel a rhythm and these tap, breaths, pushing. At the side. Of her lungs, that, that sweet bubble. Start down. In her throat.

"Ayaa natta naya," Sharda sang out across the snow.

The words of singing from our chants and our rituals and the rumble in the throat. The rumble gone to a clear tone to a note to the pure tone of the air and the lung and the woman like a beacon, like the finest hammered horn.

So many closets to singing, Sharda thought. All these singers who pretend they're not singing — women who sing with the iron sliding back and forth, the power for the song going down their arms into the metal press; singing with the broom, behind the roar of the vacuum cleaner. How many times have I sung washing dishes to hide my hands, Sharda thought? Who amongst us sing when we cook and crank up the volume to hide behind the chorus?

And yet it is *our* art. We are the wailers. The women wrote the music to communicate between the clans, the sound to glide along the hills. We wrote the songs to entertain our feet. In our guilds in the Middle Ages, a woman sang at our worktable: a good singer is a good worker, they said to her. But despite that, singing is our most belittled instrument: we cannot teach the song the way we teach the instrument. In fact, Sharda thought, I have often wanted to hold a guitar before I sing because of the way it announces you, cuts your way into the conversation, gives you a legitimacy by just holding it. The singer has no props or easy entrances. She begins, and hopes her ear has met her voice beforehand.

But to sing, to open it all and let the sound pour out until a woman is not sure where the sound comes from or where it leaves her and whether it might, perhaps, be entering her again.

Sharda kicked at the stubble. There it was, the back of the country post office, pushing up smoke through the sparse trees. The box became the focus of Sharda's attention: it had never seemed so oddly shaped, so large. She pulled the door open with a sweep, scraped her boots across the mat. She scuffed her boots absently and went to the counter in the closet-sized postal. She was stunned, having been concentrated on the journey, not the destination.

"Air Mail to Amsterdam," she said. "Think it will storm? I need to be home before dusk."